sleepover girls

Sleepover Girls is published by Capstone Young Readers
A Capstone Imprint
1710 Roe Crest Drive
North Mankato, Minnesota 56003
www.capstoneyoungreaders.com

Library of Congress Cataloging-in-Publication Data is
available on the Library of Congress website.
ISBN: 978-1-62370-305-9 (paperback)
ISBN: 978-1-4965-0542-2 (library binding)
ISBN: 978-1-4965-2351-8 (eBook)
ISBN: 978-1-62370-577-0 (eBook PDF)

Summary: It is spring break and Willow's family is heading to their
house on Whidbey Island and, for the first time, the three other
sleepover girls are coming along and Willow wants to show them
the place she loves — but once there she finds that too much
togetherness is not necessarily a good thing.

Designed by Alison Thiele

Illustrated by Paula Franco

Printed in the United States of America in Stevens Point, Wisconsin.
052015   008824WZF15

sleepover Girls

Willow's

SPRING BREAK ADVENTURE

by Jen Jones

CAPSTONE YOUNG READERS
a capstone imprint

Maren Melissa Taylor

Maren is what you'd call "personality-plus" —
sassy, bursting with energy, and always ready
with a sharp one-liner. She dreams of becoming
an actress or comedienne one day and moving
to Hollywood to make it big. Not one to fuss
over fashion, you'll often catch Maren wearing a
hoodie over a sports tee and jeans. She is an only
child, so she has adopted her friends as sisters.

Willow Marie Keys

Patient and kind, Willow is a wonderful
confidante and friend. (Just ask her twin,
Winston!) She is also a budding artist with
creativity for miles. She will definitely own
her own store one day, selling everything she
makes. Growing up in a hippie-esque family,
Willow acquired a Bohemian style that
perfectly suits her flower child within.

Delaney Ann Brand

Delaney's smart and motivated — and she's always on the go! Whether she's volunteering at the animal shelter or helping Maren with her homework, you can always count on Delaney. You'll usually spot low-maintenance Delaney in a ponytail and jeans (and don't forget her special charm bracelet, with unique charms to symbolize each one of the Sleepover Girls). She is a great role model for her younger sister, Gigi.

Ashley Francesca Maggio

Ashley is the baby of a lively Italian family.
Her older siblings (Josie, Roman, Gino, and Matt)
have taught her a lot, including how to get
attention in such a big family, which Ashley has
become a pro at. This fashionista-turned-blogger
is on top of every style trend and shares it with
the world via her blog, Magstar. Vivacious and
mischievous, Ashley is rarely sighted without
her beloved "purse puppy," Coco.

chapter One

Ahhh! I took a big whiff of the yummy-smelling rosemary oil on my wrist, hoping it would help me pay attention to the test in front of me. My mom had promised that the oil would boost my ability to focus as she'd spritzed it on me that morning. (She was hippie-dippy like that, and I loved her all the more for it.) But how was anyone supposed to focus when spring break was just a few short hours away?

It wasn't easy, that was for sure — especially since my besties and I were going to be heading to Whidbey Island. My family made the trip every year, but this was the first time I'd ever been allowed to invite anyone. Naturally, I'd invited my BFFs Ashley, Delaney, and Maren. It was going to be like one giant weeklong sleepover, and I was bursting at the seams with excitement! But first? I had to make it through midterms. (No easy task.)

With just a few minutes left of class, I buckled down to try to solve the last few pre-algebra probs. I triumphantly finished the test just as the bell started to sound.

"Woo-hoo!" I exclaimed in relief. "Oops, did I just say that out loud?"

"That you did," said Jacob Willis, striding up next to me as I gathered my stuff. "I'm pretty sure you just said what we were all feeling. So, woo-hoo right back at you!"

I tried to fight the hot blush taking over my cheeks. Jacob was my twin Winston's best friend, and for the longest time, I'd had a crush on him. But at my Halloween birthday party, I'd found out that he had a crush on my BFF Ashley. Since then, I'd been trying to see Jacob as just a friend. But much like trying to focus on math tests, it didn't always work.

I stuffed my textbook into my bag and tried to think of something witty to say. "I see I'm not the only one counting the minutes until spring break," I said, feeling a smile creep onto my face.

"Definitely not," said Jacob as we spilled out into the hallway with the rest of the class. "I'm not sure if San Francisco is ready for me and your brother!"

How lucky was Winston to be going on spring break with Jacob and his family? (Answer: so, so lucky.) Thankfully, my consolation prize was just as good — getting to take my besties on my trip! I couldn't wait to show them all the reasons I loved gorgeous, nature-rific Whidbey Island.

The thought of Whidbey Island helped me get through the day, which seemed to drag on and on. When the bell finally signaled the end of school, mass chaos broke out. People were running through the hallways, and whoops of excitement filled the air. Somehow I managed to spot Maren in the midst of all the craziness.

"I don't know what I'm more excited for — the fact that Delaney's sleepover is tonight, or the fact that we're leaving for Whidbey on Sunday," I said with a giant smile. Spring break was finally starting! "Wanna go grab a juice to celebrate?" My parents owned a health store called Creative Juices, and it was the perfect place to nab a tasty and nutritious treat!

Maren crossed her eyes and stuck out her tongue. "As tempting as a wheatgrass smoothie sounds, I've gotta go home and pack before the Little Monsters come over and tear up the place," she said. Her mom had recently gotten remarried, and her new step-sibs stayed at her house every other weekend. Needless to say, it hadn't exactly been like *The Brady Bunch* right off the bat! But she was slowly making peace with it . . . and them.

"Copy that," I told her. "Maybe you can send Alice and Ace a postcard from Whidbey Island? That would earn you big-time points with Gary."

Maren grinned. "Yeah, except most postcards say 'Wish You Were Here,' and well, I cannot tell a lie," she said in a deep George Washington voice. If her bouncy red curls were white, she probably would have looked like ol' George, too!

Before I could come up with a snappy reply, I was blinded by someone putting her hands over my eyes. "Guess who?" sang a girly voice from behind me. "I'll give you a hint. She totally finished midterms and has a hot pink suitcase that's ready to go to Whidbey Island!"

I pulled the hands off my eyes and turned around to find a very excited Ashley. Much like everyone else, she was bouncing off the walls now that spring break had begun. And I didn't blame her one bit!

"Well, well, if it isn't our very own Magstar," I said. Magstar was Ashley's super-successful fashion blog (named after her last name, Maggio). Sometimes we used it as her nickname, too.

Ashley whipped out her phone. "Oooh, that reminds me — I have to check the notifications on my latest video!" she said, eagerly scrolling through the dozens of new updates.

"Not so fast," said Maren, stealing it out of her hands. "You're on vacation, remember? I say you leave all the blog stuff behind this week and have some offline adventures!" She held the phone up high in the air so Ashley couldn't reach.

Ashley jumped up and snatched the phone back, but she put it in her jeans pocket instead of looking at it again. "I'll try, but I'm not making any promises!" she said. "I get the shakes if I'm off social media for too long."

I checked my watch for the time. "Speaking of shakes, I've gotta get to the shop," I told them. "Can one of your moms drop me off, pretty please?"

Ashley put her arm around me. "I'm sure Gino will be happy to drive you in his weirdo-wagon," she said. Her brother's beat-up blue station wagon often got us from point A to point B (but barely).

I heaved my backpack over my shoulder as we all started heading for the exit. Most of the other students were long gone. It hadn't taken long for the hallway to clear out — this place would be a ghost town for the next week.

"Luckily, we have way more reliable transportation to Whidbey," I told her. "Though going there in the Gino-mobile would definitely add to the adventure!"

Somehow, Gino managed to get me to Creative Juices in one piece. "You guys want to come in for a blueberry smoothie and a granola crunch?" I offered before getting out of the car. "It'd be on us, as a thank-you."

Gino looked like he wanted to say yes, but Ashley shut him down. "Nope, I'm gonna try to cram in a quick blog post before we all go to Delaney's tonight," she told me. "But I'll see you in a few short hours, right?"

I gave her a little salute. "You know it," I said, hopping out of the car. "Would I ever miss one of our sleepovers?"

Now that was a no-brainer. In fact, I couldn't remember any of us skipping a sleepover in all the years we'd been doing them. The closest we'd ever come was when Ashley left a sleepover early after getting in a tiff with Maren and Delaney. (I had mostly stayed out of the drama — I didn't do well with conflict.) But for the most part, every single Friday was sleepover day!

The whole tradition started back in the third grade (which, of course, felt like forever ago now that we were too-cool-for-school sixth graders). Maren's mom was editor of a travel magazine, so Maren had started sleeping over at Delaney's a lot while her mom was "on the fly." One night, they invited Ashley and me to join in the overnight fun — and the "Sleepover Girls" were born! Now we rotated houses every Friday for our weekly BFF fun.

And pretty soon, we'd be spending a whole week together! Could the world — and more importantly, my parents — handle 24/7 sleepover shenanigans? We were about to find out.

chapter Two

Maren giggled. "I have an idea. Let's play How Many Sleepover Girls Can Fit on the Bed?" she said, nudging Ashley over so she could share the pillow with her. We were all crammed onto Delaney's twin bed, reading a bunch of magazines. Delaney's dog, Frisco, was snuggled right in the middle, chewing a bully stick without a care.

Delaney scoffed. "Welcome to my world!" she said. "I'm already used to having no room in here." She glanced over at her sister Gigi's side of the room, which was currently empty since Delaney had a strict policy of no little sisters allowed at her sleepovers.

"I think it's kind of fun," I told her. "There's no one I'd rather be cozy with than you three!" I laid my head on Delaney's shoulder to prove my point. She giggled and petted me like I was Frisco.

Ashley held up the copy of *Stylish Tween* she was reading. "I have a better game," she said. "Actually, it's a quiz: 'Is He More Than Just a Friend?' Willow, this has your name all over it!"

My face turned crimson. "Um, no need to take the quiz. I already know the answer. He likes my best friend," I said, looking down.

Ashley shook her head quickly, her brown bob swinging. "No way — that was forever ago in the fall!" she said. "As far as Jacob's concerned, I'm sure I'm yesterday's news."

I wasn't so sure, but I didn't really want to talk about it. Luckily, Maren came to my rescue. "Who wants to talk about boring boys, anyway?" said Maren, snatching the issue away from Ashley. "That just might put me to sleep before midnight."

It was no shocker Maren wanted to change the subject. Up until sixth grade, she'd been completely grossed out by boys, but this year, she and Winston had been kind of a thing. However, she hated to admit it and liked to pretend she was still anti-boys.

I decided to steer the conversation toward more neutral territory — for both Maren's and my sake! "Well, we can't have you falling asleep on us," I told her. "After all, you might miss out on my special surprise."

Maren perked up. "Oooh! Drumroll, please!" she exclaimed. All of the girls started drumming their hands on their knees, Ashley's quiz already forgotten. They knew my surprises usually meant handmade gifts!

I grabbed my overnight bag and pulled out the carefully wrapped boxes that contained hand-knitted change purses. (I'd used old maps to make the wrapping paper; I figured it was too perfect for our upcoming vacay!) I'd done Ashley's purse in pink and purple, Maren's in green and white, and Delaney's in red and blue. One more project . . . *finito*!

"For my vacation vixens," I announced proudly, handing them out.

Maren tore into the map wrapping paper, while Ashley delicately took the bow off. (Knowing her, she would probably create some sort of fabulous shoelace or hair bow with it.) Delaney was first to pull her change purse out of the box.

"This is adorbs!" she exclaimed, admiring my handiwork.

Ashley and Maren loved theirs, too. "Thanks, Wills," said Maren, leaning over to give me a hug. "I'm bringing the iPod cozy you knitted for me on the trip, too. My closet is turning into the den of Willow!"

I had to laugh, because it was true — by this point, everyone had quite a collection of "Willow originals."

A loud knock came from the other side of the door. "D, let me in!" whined Gigi, fiddling with the locked doorknob. "It's time for bed, and I'm tired. I have ballet class in the morning!"

Delaney rolled her eyes. "Guess it's time for us to migrate downstairs," she said, putting all of the magazines in a neat pile. "It's not even midnight yet! We've still got plenty of mileage in this sleepover."

Actually, going to sleep didn't seem like such a bad thing right now. Midterms had totally wiped me out, and I wanted to be plenty rested when we left for Whidbey on Sunday. But it was bad form to be the first to suggest going to sleep, as any dedicated Sleepover Girl knew! So I packed up my stuff and followed the troop downstairs, where I knew more fun was in store.

Delaney was busy scrolling through the list of spring break-themed movies we could watch on Netflix when I interrupted her. "I need a little pick-me-up," I admitted. "Anyone up for a late-night snack?"

"Agreed," said Maren, leading the charge toward the kitchen. "Delaney, can we make some popcorn?" It was one of our absolute favorite sleepover snacks.

Delaney was already pulling the air popper out of the cupboard. "Not only can we make popcorn, but I'm getting out all the fixings," she said, rummaging through the rest of the cupboard. "Jalapeño salt for Maren, cinnamon sugar for Ashley, and, of course, all-natural coconut oil for Willow." A girl after my own heart! Everyone was pretty used to my health-nut ways at this point.

Soon the kernels were popping away, and we were suddenly struck with a case of the sillies. "I don't know about you guys, but I think it's been way too long since we had a kitchen dance party," said Ashley, whipping out her phone to pick a song. "After all, this midterm week was a killer. I think we need to dance!"

Pretty soon we were all dancing around the kitchen, screaming the words to every song. Even Frisco got into the spirit, running around us in circles! Maren was mid-dance move when she stopped suddenly, her eyes getting wide.

"You guys!" she said, pointing at the air popper. We'd left it on a little too long, and the kernels were overflowing everywhere! There was also a slightly burnt smell in the air.

Delaney rushed over to unplug it. "I guess that's what we get for being so corny," she said, causing all of us to fall into fits of laughter again. We really were giddy! I guessed that's what a week of impossible tests and being overexcited for spring break would do.

A loud *ahem* echoed from near the stairs, where Delaney's mom stood. Her eyes were squinty and tired, and she didn't look too happy. "I know it's spring break and all, but the music is blasting into our bedroom," she said. Her eyes shifted to the popcorn all over the floor. "And I don't even want to know how that happened."

Delaney snapped into good-daughter mode, not wanting her mom to sour on our sleepovers. "We'll make sure it's all cleaned up, Mom," she promised. Her mom raised an eyebrow. "And we'll turn down the music," Delaney added.

Delaney's mom nodded gratefully and headed back upstairs, after which we all got the giggles again. If this was what our week in Whidbey was going to be like, we were going to be having a blast 24/7!

chapter Three

Bam! Winston landed squarely on top of me, waking me out of a deep sleep. "Nothing like a body slam wake-up call," I grumbled, wriggling out from underneath him. What time was it, anyway?

"Rise and shine, blondie," said Winston, taking no pity. "Time to get your booty out of bed."

I eyed the clock next to me. It was 6:45 a.m.! "We're not leaving for two more hours!" I complained, turning over to ignore him.

Usually I was the early bird waking him up, but today it was me who could have used some extra shut-eye. I was still recovering from Delaney's epic sleepover on Friday, and last night, I'd been so excited about our trip that I'd been up tossing and turning. Plus, I liked to sleep in on vacation!

"You're not leaving yet, but I am. Jacob's going to be here any minute," said Winston. "So sue me for wanting to say goodbye to my other half."

I sat up, groggy but functional. I may have been exhausted, but I did want to say goodbye to Winston . . . and maybe see Jacob before they left. It was weird that we wouldn't be spending spring break together like we always had. "Just give me five more minutes, and I'll be downstairs — promise," I told him.

Winston grinned. "Oh, I get it. You're trying to get plenty of beauty sleep for *Jaaaacob*."

I playfully shoved him off the bed. "Don't even go there," I warned him. "Or I might have to tell Maren about the time you pooped your pants at the amusement park."

He held his hands up in surrender. "Point taken. Be downstairs in five, or I'll be back," he said in a creepy, low voice.

After pressing snooze a few more times, I stumbled downstairs in my nightgown to find the rest of my family raring to go. Outside, my dad was helping Winston load his stuff into Jacob's family's car, and my mom was bustling around the kitchen.

"Morning, Willow!" she said brightly. "After Win leaves, can you help me pack the coolers?"

We always brought tons of food to Whidbey and made most of our meals at our rental home, rather than eating out. My family was full of health nerds, so sometimes it was hard to find a menu that fit our lifestyle!

I wondered what my friends would think of my mom's morning chia smoothies and granola.

"No problem," I told her. "After all, we have plenty of time before we take off." I was still a little annoyed that Winston had interrupted my golden slumbers.

As if on cue, Winston burst through the door, followed by a hoodie-wearing Jacob. "This train is leaving the station," Winston announced. "Next stop: San Fran!"

"Yo, Willow," Jacob added, making my heart skip a beat. I immediately tried to smooth my bedhead in hopes of looking halfway decent, managing a weak *hello* back.

A few goodbye hugs (and tears shed by my mom) later, Win and Jacob were on their way, and it wasn't too much longer before Delaney showed up at our door. No shocker there — she was the most prompt person I knew!

Maren and her mom weren't far behind. After giving Delaney and me big hugs, Maren took a moment to admire our Volkswagen camper van as my dad loaded stuff into the back. "Sweet van, Mr. Keys," Maren said. "Totally retro-tastic."

The van really was a sight to see! It was totally old school, painted lime and white with a big *VW* on the front. My parents had strung Christmas lights up on the inside and decked it out with fluffy, colorful pillows and quilts. There was also a giant L-shaped seat in the back, which would be the Sleepover Girls' home for the four-hour drive!

Since Ashley was running late, everyone came inside to hang out for a little bit. My dad held everyone captive with stories about the "good ol' days," back when he and my mom drove the van cross-country to Grateful Dead concerts. I hoped this wasn't a preview of our road trip — surely my friends didn't want to spend four hours reliving my parents' hippie days! (Which had never really stopped, to be honest.)

Thankfully, it wasn't too much longer before I heard the familiar sputter of Gino's car in the driveway. I sprang up to greet them.

"Sorry we're late," called an out-of-breath Ashley. She was dressed in a blue velour jumpsuit and matching headband — the picture of comfy style. "I wanted to pre-load a bunch of blog posts before I left, and it took me forever!"

Gino smirked and pulled a giant suitcase out of the trunk. "Yeah, I'm sure it wasn't all the last-minute packing you were doing that made us late," he said. "All this stuff could clothe a small village!"

He wasn't kidding — Ash had brought two suitcases, plus an overnight tote, a big makeup case, and heaven knows what else. With the coolers, luggage for six people, and my crafting kit, it would be a tight squeeze.

"Oh, wow, Ashley, you definitely came . . . prepared," said my mom, wide-eyed. She was probably playing mental *Tetris*, trying to figure out how to fit it all in the van! Good thing my dad had added the luggage carrier.

Ashley grinned. "You know it, Mrs. K! After all, you need at least one suitcase for shoes, right?" My mom nodded, trying to be a good sport. Ashley gave Gino a look as if to say, "See? All that packing was totally necessary."

Somehow my dad managed to make it all fit, and it was finally time to get the show on the road! I wasted no time cuing up my special road-trip playlist. "Vacation, all I ever wanted, vacation, have to get away," the girls and I sang at the top of our lungs as the van pulled out of the driveway. This old '80s tune by the Go-Gos was too perfect!

A few minutes later, Maren leaned over and lightly punched my arm. "Slug bug!" she yelled, pointing out the window at a bright yellow Volkswagen Beetle.

Delaney looked confused. "What the heck is a slug bug?" she asked.

Maren grinned. "You're supposed to yell, 'Slug bug,' and slug someone every time you see a Beetle," she shared. "It's a road trip must." She'd had plenty of experience with road trips, thanks to her mom's love of travel.

I started scanning for Beetles as my dad pulled onto the freeway. "Well, in that case, the next Bug I see, it's on!"

Delaney pulled out a notepad. "Until then, I think we should make the most of our time in the car," she said. "Let's make a bucket list for everything we want to do in Whidbey!"

We were all game to play along — Delaney always kept us on task with her organized ways.

"Here's mine," I volunteered. "I want to show you guys my secret place." I'd found it several years back on a walk through the woods. It was the most peaceful, most gorgeous spot on the island.

"A secret place?" said Maren. "Count me in." A natural drama queen, she loved anything secret or suspenseful. Delaney and Ashley nodded excitedly. They, too, were always up for new adventures.

I turned my attention over to Delaney. "What about you, D?" I asked.

Delaney looked pretty excited. "I read that there's an old drive-in movie theater on the island," she said. "I'd love to check it out!"

My mom swiveled around from the front seat. "Lucky you," she said. "It's on the agenda already. We thought it would be the perfect place to take the ol' VW van." Delaney did a little fist pump to show her approval.

We kept brainstorming more bucket list stuff. Ashley wanted to go to the beach, and Maren wanted to find an amazing souvenir for her mom. (Her mom was always bringing back cool stuff from her world travels, so Maren figured it was time to return the favor.)

With our bucket list decided, Ashley started a game of Alphabet Soup. The idea was to spot signs or landmarks starting with each letter of the alphabet. We decided that whoever got the letters Q and X would get extra points. It was kind of fun playing — Washington was so pretty! It was a treat just to stare out the window.

By the time we got to Q, we were all hot on the lookout. I squinted, trying to read a faraway billboard. Did it say what I thought it did? I grabbed my binoculars out of my bag to be sure.

"Aha!" I yelled triumphantly. "Quizno's Subs, baby. Who's the queen of Alphabet Soup?"

Ashley grinned and put an imaginary tiara on my head. "I officially crown you new reigning champion of Alphabet Soup," she said. "Until we get to X. Then I'm stealing my title back."

Soon we started to see signs for Seattle, which gave us an easy S (and got us excited, because it meant we were getting even closer!). Maren directed our attention to a giant landmark in the distance. "Look!" she said. "Isn't that the Space Needle?"

Everyone crowded around for a better look. I stayed back so they could see better — after all, my family had made this drive a million times! We never did find an X (take that, Ashley!), but as we neared Whidbey Island, I saw something even better: the sign for the Clinton-Mulkiteo ferry. It was official. We were just one short sail away from spring break . . . and I couldn't wait.

chapter Four

"I'm the queen of the world!" yelled Maren, opening her arms out wide. She and I leaned against the rail to look over the water, and Maren's red curls blew in the breezy air as the ferry sailed closer to Whidbey Island. She was quoting one of our fave movies, *Titanic*, which we'd watched a bazillion times at our sleepovers.

It really was a sight to see. The greenish-blue waters of the Puget Sound stretched out endlessly before us. In the distance, I could see the lush trees of Whidbey Island. Beyond that were gorgeous snow-capped mountains that looked like they were straight out of *The Sound of Music*! I was so excited to be able to share the awesomeness of this area with my friends.

Speaking of friends . . . where were my other two BFFs? We hadn't seen Delaney or Ash in a while. My parents had left us all on the deck while they went out to eat; I couldn't blame them after being stuck in the car with us.

We found Delaney soon enough; she was at the snack bar grabbing us some munchies (a fruit plate for me and caramel corn for everyone else). She hadn't seen Ash, either, so we scouted around for her. After searching all over the deck, we found her inside the cabin, glued to her smartphone!

"Here you are!" said Delaney, who spotted Ashley first.

Ashley grimaced. "Sorry, the only place I could get Wi-Fi was in here. I remembered I still had a few more things to do for Magstar," she explained.

Maren snatched the phone away from her and grinned. "Didn't we have this talk already?" she reminded Ash. "This is your week to say *sayonara* to social media."

I grabbed Ashley's hand to pull her up from the seat. "Come on, you're missing a killer view!" I urged. "Let's go get a pic of all of us — you can even post it to Instagram if you want."

That perked Ashley up. "Let's do it! I can see the hashtag now: #sleepovergirlsonspringbreak."

It always cracked me up the way Ashley narrated her life in hashtags. I wondered how she would survive a whole week away from her laptop! But luckily, we had plenty of fun plans in store to keep her occupied (or so I hoped, as it wouldn't be fun without her).

We took our group selfie, and before we knew it, the boat was pulling into the dock at Whidbey Island. "How cute!" said Ashley, pointing at the rows of colorful houses along the water. I was glad she'd looked up from her smartphone long enough to see them.

But I couldn't wait for her to see our house. Well, it wasn't ours, exactly, but we rented it every spring break, so it felt like it. The house was located right on the water, with a tiny little private beach. There was also a fire pit in the backyard and a deck with a hot tub! Inside the house, there were tons of skylights and windows, which meant bright sunlight and amazing views of the water. In a nutshell: heaven.

We had to wait in a pretty long line to get our van back and leave the ferry station. But once on the windy drive over to our house, my stomach started fluttering. I'd been looking forward to this since forever! My dad seemed excited, too, pointing out all of his favorite places along the way.

"Look, there's the old lighthouse!" exclaimed Delaney, getting in the spirit. You could tell she'd done her research. "I've heard it's haunted by the ghost of a dead captain . . . boo!" She grabbed Maren by the shoulders, trying to scare her.

But tough Maren wasn't spooked so easily. "*Oooh*, maybe we should go ghost hunting one night," she said, her eyes lighting up.

My mom piped in from the front seat. "I don't think you guys will be going anywhere at night by yourselves," she reminded everyone. "We'll have to go over some ground rules once we get to the house."

Kind of embarrassing, but on the other hand, I was relieved. Maren may have been super brave, but I, on the other hand, was not.

Going ghost hunting sounded about as much fun as being a third wheel on a date with Jacob and Ashley.

As the van finally stopped in the house's pebble-filled driveway, Maren clapped her hands in excitement. "We're here! We're here!" she exclaimed, bouncing up and down in her seat.

"Yep, and only forty-five 'Are we there yets?' later," Delaney teased. Maren had mild ADHD and did not enjoy sitting still for hours at a time.

Maren didn't bother answering — she was too busy hopping out of the van and running down to the shore to see the water. The sun was already starting to set, and the sky looked amazing with streaks of pink, purple, and orange.

"Willow, this is totally gorge," Ashley said, taking it all in. "Talk about a perfect Insta photo!" She snapped a photo with her phone, but quickly frowned as she tried to post it. "Oh, I have no signal out here. Is there Wi-Fi in the house?"

I wasn't sure. "Why don't we go settle in, and we can find out?" I suggested. My family usually unplugged when we were up here, and using any sort of electronic device was usually the furthest thing from our minds.

After I gave a quick tour of the house, we settled into our bedrooms. I was bunking up with Maren, and Delaney and Ashley were rooming together. I threw my suitcase on the bed and then noticed an envelope with my name on it and a book on top of the pillow.

I tore the envelope open curiously. "Dear Willow," it read. "We know how much you love art. Please enjoy this book of watercolors and let it inspire you as you spend time on the island! Sincerely, The Huntley Family." Underneath the card was a book titled *Watercolors of Whidbey* with lots of paintings done by local artists. How sweet! The family who owned the house was always leaving us fun little surprises.

Maren peered over my shoulder. "Awesome, Wills!" she said. "I think we should go outside and get one last look at that awesome sunset. You know, for artistic inspiration." She was bouncing off the walls.

I grinned. "I've got an even better idea," I said. "Let's go hot tubbing, and we can watch the sun disappear from there!"

Maren and I went to get Ashley and Delaney, and pretty soon we were all in our swimsuits enjoying the hot bubbles. It was such a relaxing end to a long (but fun) day. I leaned my head back and shut my eyes for a minute, loving the fact that I was living the good life with my three besties.

The screen door opened, and my mom appeared with a tray of mint lemonades. "Thought you guys could use a drink," she said, leaving it on the ledge. "We still have about forty-five minutes before dinner, so feel free to hang out here for a while." My parents could be pretty cool when they wanted to be. (Or maybe they just wanted us out of their hair for a little bit!)

Delaney grabbed one of the lemonades and hoisted it into the air. "Now we can check hot tubbing off the bucket list!" she said. "And here's to Willow for making this amazing trip happen."

chapter Five

"Wake up, Sleeping Beauty!" called Delaney, peeping her head in the doorway. "We've got a long day ahead of us, and I don't want to waste a minute!"

A little groggy, I rolled over to see if Maren was still sleeping, but she was long gone. "Where's Maren?" I asked.

Delaney sat down on the bed. "She went on an early morning bike ride," she told me. "And your dad's trying to help Ashley set up the Wi-Fi downstairs." Ash was definitely on a mission!

I followed Delaney downstairs, where my dad and Ashley had their heads buried in the instruction manual for the router. My mom was making oatmeal pancakes with vegan maple "bacon." My kind of breakfast!

"Morning, everyone," I said, still trying to wake up. The girls and I had stayed up late last night, playing card games and watching movies.

My mom filled us in on her plans for the day while Delaney and I helped set the breakfast table for everyone. "So first I was thinking we could walk around Langley a little bit and explore," she told us. "And then we can have a late picnic lunch outside. It's so warm today, so we might as well take advantage of it!"

The temperatures on Whidbey Island were usually in the fifties and sixties in March, but today it was supposed to be a balmy sixty-eight degrees! Walking around the cute little town of Langley seemed like a good idea, too. Delaney would probably love the bookstore, Ashley would go crazy over the boutiques, and Maren could definitely find a super cool souvenir somewhere. As for me, I'd definitely pop into a few of the art galleries! There would be something for everyone.

Then Maren burst through the screen door, out of breath but smiling. "You didn't tell me how hilly it was around here!" she said, bending over to catch her breath. "This place has more mounds than a BMX course."

"Good to know," said Delaney. "I'll have to map out some easy routes for when we ride our bikes into town." That was Delaney — always wanting to be prepared!

Keeping the hilly terrain in mind, we decided to take the V-Dubs (as Ashley had lovingly named our Volkswagen van) into Langley that afternoon. It was tough finding a parking space big enough, but my dad managed to do it.

"Okay, it's ten-thirty now," said my dad, checking his watch. "Why don't we meet back here at the van at twelve-thirty, and then we'll head to lunch?" I was excited that my parents were letting us go off and explore on our own.

The first store that caught my eye was called "Knitty Purls." Immediately, I was dying to go inside.

"Can we check it out?" I begged the girls. "I used up pretty much all of my yarn making the change purses, and I would love to see what they have."

Everyone was game. Inside was like a yarn wonderland! I picked out a really cool tie-dye silk one, as well as one called Whidbey Gems that captured the beautiful blue and green shades around the island.

Ashley peeked over my shoulder to see which yarns I'd picked. "I think this store is a Whidbey gem," she said. "Wills, will you teach me how to knit? I could definitely save tons of money if I started making my own clothes."

"You got it," I said. "I'll make you a deal — I'll show you how to knit if you show me how to set up an Etsy store." We did a little fist bump to seal the deal. If anyone could help me bring my art to the online masses, it was Ash.

Next we spotted a place called Myken's, which was the cutest pet shop ever! Delaney and Ashley were all over that, since Frisco and Coco were at the top of their shopping lists.

It didn't take Delaney long to find an adorable plaid doggie raincoat. "Oh my!" she said, holding it up so we could all see it better. "This is perfect for Frisco. He gets so wet every time it rains!" I was surprised she didn't have one already — Valley View could be pretty rainy in the winter months. Thankfully, spring was right around the corner.

Meanwhile, Ashley had found her own objects of affection: a totally blinged-out doggie collar and a tiny red beret. "Which one do you like more?" she said, holding them up.

Maren pointed at the beret. "I think Coco already has enough bling to make Paris Hilton jealous," she said. "Definitely the beret, all the way."

Ashley agreed, and after she and Delaney made their purchases, we checked out a few clothing shops and a store full of yummy-smelling soaps. I was about to lead everyone into my favorite store, a really artsy place called Nymbol's Secret Garden, when Ashley stopped and checked the time.

"Do you guys mind if I duck into the coffee shop and meet you at the van?" she asked, looking a little guilty. "I want to check my

Twitter feed and a few other things on my phone." I was a little bummed, but we all agreed to meet back at the V-Dubs.

So we split up. Ashley went to the coffee place, and Maren, Delaney, and I headed to Nymbol's Secret Garden. It felt a little weird to not have Ashley with us, but Maren ended up finding an awesome dream catcher made out of twigs for her mom, so we were glad we'd gone in!

Back at the van, my parents weren't thrilled that Ashley had left the group. They gave us a little lecture but were glad we were all back safe and sound. Once we were all buckled in, it was off to the winery for lunch! Picnicking at the winery was a family tradition, and I hoped my friends would love it as much as I did.

After my parents bought a bottle of wine, we set up shop at a picnic table in the apple orchard, where you could look out at all of the grapes growing on the vines. Practically a postcard! I texted Winston a quick pic to show him what he was missing.

"This is *sooooo* pretty, Mr. and Mrs. Keys," said Ashley, echoing my thoughts. She seemed to have left the digital world behind after her coffee shop detour.

Delaney grabbed one of the sandwiches out of the cooler my mom had brought. "Yep," she said, "the scenery's great and all, but this sandwich is a sight for sore eyes." She eagerly tore off the wrapping and took a giant bite.

She had a point — we were all pretty hungry. My mom set out a little fruit and cheese plate, along with all of the sandwiches she'd premade, and we gobbled them up in record time. "So much for a leisurely picnic," said my mom with a laugh. "Someone call the *Guinness Book of World Records*!"

Maren patted her belly, satisfied. "I've got a good way to work off the calories," she said with a grin. "Anyone up for a game of hide-and-seek in the vineyards?"

Ashley wrinkled her nose. "Aren't we a little old for hide-and-seek? We're going to be in seventh grade soon!"

Maren looked a little bummed, so Delaney jumped in. "Exactly," said Delaney. "So we only have a few months left to act like little kids! Might as well take advantage of it." She started tickling Ashley until she gave in.

And I was glad to see it. Not too long ago, we'd had a blast playing flashlight tag at one of my sleepovers. It'd be a bummer if any of us were suddenly too "cool" to do the same goofy stuff we'd always done! "You guys are on," I told them, polishing off my roasted veggie sandwich. "And guess what, Ashley . . . you're it!" And the vacation vixens were off to the vines.

chapter Six

It was already Wednesday, and the week was flying by way too quickly. So far everyone had been getting along fine — sure, Delaney had her bossy moments, Maren could get a little restless, and Ashley was having a hard time unplugging, but overall, we were having a blast! I was sure today's kayak outing would be no exception.

But after we'd been out on the water for a bit, things got a little "choppy." Delaney and Maren weren't having the easiest time propelling their kayak over the waves.

"You have to follow what I'm doing!" Delaney grumbled at Maren. "I'm sitting in front, so I can't see how you're paddling."

The two of them were drifting farther and farther away from the rest of us. They just couldn't seem to get their paddling motions in sync! This morning's kayak jaunt was supposed to be relaxing, but their bickering was starting to put a damper on things.

"The person in back is supposed to be the anchor," argued Maren. "That means I lead the way we're paddling." She put her oar in her lap dramatically, as if to say, "I give up."

My mom and dad paddled closer to them so they could show them the right technique. "Here, try it like this," my mom said gently, showing them how to row in tandem. "You'll get a lot farther that way!"

Delaney and Maren imitated their motions, and pretty soon, they were gliding over the water. As they got closer to me and Ashley, I gave them an encouraging grin. "See, it's all about being Zen," I said, gesturing to all of the nature around us. "Try to enjoy your time in the great outdoors!" Delaney just grunted in response.

"Listen to Mother Willow," joked Ashley. "She knows best." She gave them a playful splash with her oar to lighten the mood.

Maren leaned over to return the favor, but the kayak ended up flipping and she and Delaney plunged into the water! "Ack!" Delaney sputtered. She started flailing her arms to try to keep the kayak from drifting away.

Ashley clapped her hands over her mouth, trying to cover a giggle. "Oops," she said. "My bad."

"Oh, real hilarious, Ash!" said Maren, who was now treading water. "Don't make me tip you in here with us."

Ashley paddled our kayak out of reach, not wanting to risk her carefully braided hairdo. Sensing the tension, my dad rowed in between us to prevent any further overboard incidents. "Why don't we head back?" he proposed. "I think we've had enough excitement out here for today."

No one could argue with that, so we headed back toward dry land. My dad bought us all hot chocolates so we could warm up — especially soggy Maren and Delaney!

"A little whipped cream, Ash?" asked Maren, spraying a dollop onto Ashley's nose. Maren wasn't going to forget their accidental plunge anytime soon.

Luckily, Ashley took it in stride and licked it right off. "Thanks, M," she joked. "You can never have too much whipped cream for your hot chocolate."

"Well, maybe there's a thing such as too much togetherness," huffed Delaney, wrapping a blanket around herself to warm up. "You won't find me on a kayak with Maren again any time soon!"

My face fell. This morning had kind of been a disaster. All I wanted was for everyone to fall in love with Whidbey the way I had, but it didn't help when everyone was bickering! Had we hit a turning point? Usually we got along awesome, but we'd never spent more than a few days together before. Was Delaney right about too much togetherness?

"Earth to Willow," said Maren, waving her hand in front of my face. "Ready to go? We need to head home and shower so we can make it to the drive-in on time."

I tried to shake it off. "You know it," I said, following her into the van. The drive-in was going old school tonight and showing *Grease*, and it was sure to be a blast! Maybe catching a fun flick could help turn the day around.

We managed to rotate our way through taking showers (no easy feat for a group of six). Ashley even let Delaney and Maren go first, which I thought was a good sign. Usually, she needed tons of time to get ready. It seemed like everyone was getting along peachy again. But then, right before we were all going to leave, Ashley dropped the bomb. She wanted to stay home and catch up on social media stuff.

Maren slung her arm around Ashley's shoulder. "Oh, come on, Maggio," she urged. "I promise I won't give you the whipped cream treatment again. In fact, I'll even buy you some Junior Mints to make up for it. Pinky swear!"

"Yeah, and you won't have to listen to me and Maren fight anymore," promised Delaney.

Ashley shook her head. "That's so sweet, guys, but it has nothing to do with today," she told us. "I just need my online fix! I'll just skip this one thing. Is that cool?"

So we were off to the Blue Fox Drive-In —
minus one Sleepover Girl and my dad, who
stayed home with Ashley. (He was probably
relieved not to have to watch *Grease*, too.) I was
bummed, but I knew Ashley had been going a
bit crazy being "off the grid." Might as well let
her do her thing.

The familiar sight of the drive-in cheered me
up, with rows of cars already lined up to watch the
movie. The sky was a dark cobalt blue, providing
a dramatic backdrop for the movie screen. It was
one of my fave places on the island, and I knew
Delaney and Maren would love it, too!

Maren took it all in while we were setting up
our lawn chairs. "You didn't tell me there was
a go-kart track here!" said Maren, nudging me.

"I think it's closed at night," I told her. "But
there's an arcade — want to go check that
out before the movie starts?" Maren nodded
excitedly; she was always up for video games.

Plus, she probably didn't want to sit around waiting for the movie to start.

Maren and I grabbed Delaney and headed into the loud arcade, which was filled with kids running around and being crazy. Guess we weren't the only spring breakers here to let loose! "*Oooh*, look, a fortune-telling machine," I said, pointing at a gypsy mannequin inside a giant case. "We have to do that."

Delaney's eyes lit up, but Maren looked a little skeptical. "Be my guest," she said. "I'm saving my quarters for the pinball machine!"

"Here goes nothing," I said, plunking a quarter in the slot. The machine lit up, and the fake gypsy's eyes rolled back in her head as she waved her hands in the air. A tiny paper fortune came out of the slot, and I picked it up eagerly. "Stormy skies lie ahead . . ." read the sheet.

Seeing my frowny face, Delaney read over my shoulder. "Well, that's not exactly a rosy fortune," she said. "Here, let me try." She put in a quarter, and the fortune was exactly the same! I was weirded out, but Delaney just giggled. "See, it's probably broken or something," she assured me.

"Yeah," I said, trying to sound happier than I felt.

Maren took my hand. "C'mon, who needs stupid fortune tellers when you can take on the Big Kahuna?" she said, leading us toward a game that forced players to balance on a surfboard or be tossed onto an inflatable "ocean" wave. "I need to redeem myself after today's poor showing on the water."

Now THAT I had to see. I crumpled up the fortune, threw it into the trash, and followed Maren. I was determined to have a great night — with no storms in the forecast.

chapter Seven

A few hours later, I was in much better spirits after watching one of my fave flicks with two of my besties. After all, how could you not be in a good mood after a few hours at the drive-in? My mom slipped the key into the door as we sang songs from the movie at the top of our lungs.

My mom raised her hand to her lips to shush us. "Girls, it's getting late," she warned. "You don't want to wake Dad and Ashley."

A voice piped up from the living room. "Are you kidding me?" said Ashley. "I'm wide awake. I've been dying for you guys to get home!" My dad, on the other hand, wasn't so peppy; he was snoring away on the recliner. It felt good to know Ash had missed us. Even though we'd had a lot of fun at the drive-in, it would have been even better with her there.

"Good thing, *dahling*, because the night is young," said Maren in a cheesy voice. That could mean only one thing: sleepover-style fun was in store! This day was ending on a much better note than it started.

"I'm glad you all have so much energy, but these two old fogies are going to bed," said my mom, nudging my dad to wake him up. "Can I get you guys some kale treats or granola balls before we head upstairs?"

"Sounds tempting, Mom, but I think we'll make some ice cream sundaes instead," I told her. Delaney gave me a grateful smile. She and the rest of the girls were probably getting tired of all the healthy stuff! The Keys diet wasn't for everyone.

My parents groggily headed upstairs while we sprawled out on the sectional couch. "So what did I miss?" said Ashley, bouncing up and down on the couch. "I ended up being on my computer for only a little while, and then I just sat here reading *Stylish Tween* and listening to the crickets."

"Hashtag #WhidbeyProbs," said Delaney, teasing her. "Guess you should have come with us to the drive-in after all!"

Delaney and I started to fill her in on our arcade adventures and what the drive-in was like, but now it was Maren's turn to have her head buried in her phone. We all looked at her curiously when she started giggling.

"Check this out," she said, holding up her phone. It was a text from Winston — no surprise there! The two of them had been texting back and forth all week. Winston had sent a picture of him cracking an egg over Jacob's head. It said, "Don't stay up too late tonight! After all, we heard you got up at the 'crack' of dawn this morning to go kayaking."

The other girls started laughing, but I just buried my head in my hands. "That twin of mine," I said, smiling despite myself. "A real keeper, that one!"

Maren laughed. "I really know how to pick 'em. Well, one ridiculous text deserves another, don't you think?" Sassy Maren always made sure she had the last word.

She gathered us all into a tight cluster so we could take a group selfie. "Say cheese!" she instructed, snapping the photo. Then she applied some sort of filter that made us look all weird and distorted, typing in, "Good idea, genius! We're so tired we can barely see straight."

Delaney grabbed the phone from her hand to see the photo. "We look like we belong in a funhouse!" she said, barely containing her giggles. She made a funny face to try to match the one in the picture. Ashley followed suit. Pretty soon, we were all trying to top each other with our "funhouse faces."

After a few minutes, we were all out of breath from laughing so hard. "I don't know about you guys, but I'm feeling pretty lightheaded," I told them. "Want to go outside and get some fresh air?"

"I've got an even better idea," said Delaney, eyeing some empty mason jars on the table. "Let's go catch fireflies! There are tons of them out there tonight."

"Heck yeah!" exclaimed Ashley. "I've been cooped up all night. Just let me grab my hoodie."

Whew — felt like things were getting back to normal. Delaney led the charge outside, where the brisk air awaited and the sound of the crickets coming from the woods was almost overwhelming. We all took a silent moment to stare out at the peaceful water, which was lapping over the rocks on the beach. After a few minutes, Maren giggled and said, "We're not in Valley View anymore, are we, Toto?"

"Far from it," agreed Ashley. "This place is so romantic! I bet you're wishing ol' Winston was here." Mischievous Ashley could never resist the chance to bring up boys.

Maren rolled her eyes. "Very funny," she said. But she didn't deny it for once! Their shared crush was pretty much out in the open now. Maybe they'd get married one day, and Maren would be my sister-in-law! But who was I kidding? We were pretty much sisters already.

Delaney echoed my thoughts. "What will I do without you guys next week? This trip is going way too fast," she said. She did a little cartwheel, collapsing onto the grass.

"It's not like we won't see each other at school," Ashley reminded her, making another "funhouse face" to show just what she thought about that.

Maren pretended to gag. "Don't say the *S* word!" she warned. "I'm content to pretend I'll be on spring break for the rest of my life." She ran into the yard to catch a neon firefly with her jar, and we all followed suit. This was the kind of stuff that lit me up on the inside! Cheesy, but totally true.

chapter Eight

"Could you pass the quinoa?" asked Ashley, reaching for the heaping bowl my mom had made. It seemed like my friends were starting to come around to the healthier side of things after spending the week with my family!

I handed the bowl over. "Seconds, huh?" I teased her. "Next thing you know, you're going to be craving all these crazy healthy foods when we get back."

Even the mere mention of going back home made me feel sad. It was hard to believe the week was already more than half over! We'd spent today exploring this really cool place called Earth Sanctuary. It was a sculpture garden in the forest, and they even had a labyrinth that you could walk through. My fave part was seeing all the wildlife and spotting a bald eagle, an owl, and even a river otter! So cute.

Ashley put a huge helping of quinoa on her spoon with a grin. "Stranger things have happened," she admitted.

"Speaking of strange and spooky, I have a little surprise for you guys," said my dad, whipping out six paper tickets. "Tonight we're going on the 'Haunted Whidbey' tour!"

Maren's eyes lit up. "So we're going ghost hunting for reals? Rock on, Mr. K!" She, Delaney, and Ashley started high-fiving in excitement, but I slumped down into my chair. As Winston was always saying, I was the biggest scaredy-cat ever — and he was right.

"Um, I think I'll stay home and work on Ashley's blog?" I joked, knowing they would never let me miss out on the haunted hijinks.

Delaney patted my shoulder nicely. "Don't worry, we'll protect you, Wills," she promised with a grin. My friends knew I was usually the first one to hide under the blanket when we watched scary movies!

Somehow I still found myself at the Captain Whidbey Inn with everyone else at seven o'clock sharp. What had I gotten myself into? The tour guide greeted us with a creepy grin as we entered the lobby along with the other unsuspecting tour-goers.

"Welcome to one of the most haunted spots on Whidbey Island," said the tour guide, letting out what I guessed was supposed to be a scary cackle.

"I think she's pretty scary herself," Maren whispered in my ear, trying to put me at ease. With Maren around, it would be hard not to stay in good *spirits*. (Pun intended!)

Our guide, whose name was Maeve, led us down the supposedly haunted hallway to start the tour. First stop? Room six, where the ghost of Joseph Whidbey's wife was known to roam.

"Remind me not to stay here any time soon," I whispered to Delaney as we listened to Maeve share the scary story. She nodded silently, caught up in what Maeve was saying.

As we kept walking through the hotel, Maeve pointed out other rooms known for spooky sightings and unexplained noises.

"In this room, people have seen unexplained outlines of people imprinted into the bed," said Maeve, motioning toward the bed.

Just then, the lights flickered, and I accidentally let out a little shriek. Everyone on the tour turned to look at me, and I gave an embarrassed grin.

Maeve laughed. "You haven't seen anything yet! Wait until we reach Ebey's Landing!"

As it turned out, Ebey was one of the first settlers on Whidbey Island, and his headless ghost was known to haunt the exact spot where he was killed.

"You doing all right, Willow Bean?" asked my dad, noticing how freaked out I was. The tour van pulled up next to a log cabin at Sunnyside Cemetery. I braced myself against the seat.

"Sorry, guys, but I draw the line here," I told my friends. "No way am I going into a cemetery." I didn't usually speak up for myself, and I hated causing drama, but this was too much.

Maren pouted. "Come on, Wills! Don't you want to try to spot the ghost of Isaac Ebey?"

My mom put her hand on my shoulder. "I'll stay with you in the van, Willow," she said.

I didn't want to seem like a baby. Everyone else seemed so jazzed about checking it out, even the little kids on the tour! "No, you guys go ahead," I told them. "I'll just read stuff on my phone or something."

My mom wasn't convinced, so she ended up staying with me while Dad, the girls, and the rest of the group went off to learn more about Ebey and his gruesome past.

Secretly, I was grateful that she'd stayed. Sitting alone near a cemetery? No thanks! We were talking quietly when I thought I heard something in the distance.

I shifted uncomfortably. "Did you hear that?" I asked my mom. She tried to pretend she hadn't heard anything, but it looked like she'd heard it, too.

Soon, the creepy voice called out again. "*Ebeyyyyyyyyy,*" it said, getting louder. This time, my mom couldn't deny hearing it. I buried my head in her shoulder, wishing that the rest of the group would get back already.

The voice came a few more times, to the point that I was legit scared out of my mind. All of a sudden, three heads popped up against the van window.

"EBEY!" screamed Maren, Ashley, and Delaney. I jumped, my heart beating a million miles a minute. Then the tears I'd been holding back started streaming down my face — totally embarrassing! And totally not cool of my friends, since they knew how scared I was. So much for them having my back!

chapter Nine

The next morning, I skipped breakfast and stayed in my room. Maren had slept in Delaney and Ashley's room, probably because they'd stayed up late and she didn't want to wake me. (Or maybe she knew how upset I was?) I, on the other hand, had gone to bed as soon as we got home. The sooner I could forget the night's events, the better! It had been an awkward and quiet ride home. Plus, my mom had given the girls a stern lecture, which had been pretty embarrassing.

Curled up on the window seat, I watched the rain pouring down outside, which felt like a perfect match for my mood. However, the weather didn't bode well for the bucket list item I'd had in mind for today — taking the girls to my secret place. Maybe it was for the best. I didn't really feel like hanging out with them right now, anyway.

But a loud knock on the door told me I didn't really have a choice. "Calling Ms. Willow Keys!" came Ashley's voice. "We have a special delivery for you."

The door opened, and the three of them came in, carrying a tray full of breakfast pastries and my favorite green juice.

"It's the three ghosts of Whidbey past," joked Maren, setting the tray down in front of me. "Can you forgive us for being so incredibly stupid?"

"You know we love you, Wills," Delaney said.

"We just got caught up in the moment and figured you'd think it was funny."

I took a small bite of a kale-and-cheese croissant. "It's okay. I was really freaked out, but I know you'd never scare me or be mean on purpose. So it's time to forgive and forget," I told them. "But next time, let's leave old Ebey in the cemetery where he belongs! Deal?"

"You mean, *Ebeyyyyyy*?" joked Ashley, but at my look, she backed down.

Delaney wisely changed the subject. "So, since it's raining today, we thought we could stay in and do something you would enjoy, Willow," she said.

Ashley piped in. "You mean, rather than the super long itinerary you originally planned for us today?" she teased. Delaney had been determined to make the most of our last day on the island and had a mile-long to-do list to show for it.

Delaney stuck her tongue out at Ashley, then turned to face me. "So, will you get dressed and meet us downstairs for a little surprise?"

I gestured at my fleece pjs. "Get dressed? No need! Rainy days are what pajamas are for," I said, laughing and taking a sip of my green juice. "Let's go."

When I went downstairs, I saw that the girls had set up the dining room table to do one of my favorite things: nature crafts! My heart melted just a little.

"See, Wills, you can't be mad at us," said Maren, holding up a giant pinecone. "Delaney made us go out and pick all these pinecones in the pouring rain this morning."

I giggled. "The things we do for friendship. What are we making?"

Delaney pulled out her iPad to show me the project they'd picked. "We thought we could make a door wreath and leave it for the Huntleys," she said.

"I love it!" I was so impressed with their thoughtfulness, especially after last night.

Delaney turned on some tunes, and we were off to a good start, spray-painting the cones a glittery gold color and hot gluing them onto the wreath. (I knew my crafting kit would come in handy!) But it was taking a long time, and about halfway through the project, Ashley and Maren seemed to lose interest. Ash kept paging through an issue of *Stylish Tween* and checking her Instagram, and Maren was texting Winston.

"Come on, ladies, these cones aren't going to glue themselves," said Delaney.

Maren gave her a sarcastic salute. "Yes, bossypants!" she said, putting down her phone.

Delaney looked hurt. "Just trying to keep everyone focused, that's all," she said. "If that's a crime, I guess I'm guilty." She suddenly seemed to be really interested in the pinecone she was gluing.

"Well, sometimes you act like it's a crime

if we're not all on your agenda," said Ashley, backing up Maren. Uh-oh.

Delaney folded her arms. "Since when is it Gang Up on Delaney Day? We're supposed to be enjoying our last day together, and you are spoiling it!"

I swallowed nervously. This was starting to get out of hand. "Guys, I —"

But Maren cut me off. "Well, it's a little hard to enjoy yourself when you've been cooped up inside from the rain all day, and the only thing to do is glue down a bunch of silly pinecones," Maren replied, her voice getting louder. "I'm just going a little stir-crazy, that's all."

"Surprise, surprise," muttered Delaney. "Maybe you and Ashley should go to the coffee shop so you can use their precious Wi-Fi!"

Their bickering started getting louder and louder. I couldn't take it anymore. I pushed my chair back and ran up the steps to my room. I wanted nothing to do with all this fighting and drama. I just wanted to have the perfect spring break with my friends. But this vacation had started going downhill fast, and I wasn't sure how to stop it. Maybe the fortune had been right. The skies were stormy — both outside and inside.

My friends softly knocked on my door again, but this time I didn't answer. I was waiting for the skies to clear up, and I knew exactly where I would go: my happy place, a.k.a. my secret place. And I would go by myself.

chapter Ten

An hour later, the rain clouds finally parted, and I was ready to head outside. All was quiet downstairs — maybe the girls were taking a nap? That was fine with me; I needed some time on my own. I hated it when we all fought.

I found my dad reading a book on the porch swing. "Going on a hike, Dad," I told him, taking a second to put on my rain boots.

He gave me a knowing look. "Okay, honey," he said. "Your mom took the girls into town so everyone could cool down a bit. Will you be okay on your own?"

"Yeah, I'll be fine," I assured him. I'd made this hike by myself a million times, but it was cute that he still felt the need to ask.

"Well, bring your phone just in case you need to call for any reason," he added.

I nodded obediently. "Will do," I promised.

With that, I headed into the woods next to our house, the leaves crinkling and crunching under my feet. As I got deeper into the trees, I started to feel calmer. Other than the occasional rustle of a squirrel or the sound of the ferry in the distance, it felt perfectly peaceful. Here I was, in the middle of a magical forest on Whidbey Island.

After a few more twists and turns, I came to an opening and was rewarded with the final destination: my secret place!

I let out a deep breath as I took it all in. It was just as I remembered it. The leaves on the trees were so vivid they were almost neon green. A gentle, rolling creek sparkled in the sunlight. Right over the creek rested a huge log where you could just sit and relax.

And that was exactly what I planned to do — while I was painting, of course! I'd grabbed my art kit and a blank canvas, as well as the book the Huntleys had given me. I'd barely had time to read through it, and after being so busy with doing things with my friends, I definitely had the artistic itch.

I flipped through the book, admiring the way other artists had portrayed the area. Pretty soon, my paintbrush was gliding over the canvas, and I was in the creative groove. With each brushstroke, I felt my frustration over the last few days fade away. It was the best stress relief I could get, and I really needed it.

By the time my painting was complete, the sun had shifted and just a few streaks of light were passing through the trees. I hated to say it, but it was time to go back. I took a second to admire my finished product.

My secret place was now captured for the world (or at least my friends) to see. Leaving the woods, I had a little skip in my step and felt a lot more like myself. I let out a happy sigh. A little alone time was exactly what I had needed.

Back at the house, I found everyone in the backyard crowding around the fire pit. The girls rushed up to give me a hug when they spotted me emerging from the woods.

"Willow!" the girls cried in unison, which seemed a little dramatic.

"We feel so bad that you went by yourself," said Delaney. "I know taking us to your secret place was one of your bucket list things. I'm so sorry for how today went down."

"Yeah, we didn't mean to start arguing," said Ashley. "I guess we got possessed by the ghost of Ebey! It won't happen again."

Maren handed me a stick with some marshmallows on it so I could join them in making s'mores. "A peace offering?" she said.

I accepted the peace offering gladly. "No prob at all. I love you girls to the ends of the earth, but maybe the occasional break from each other isn't such a bad thing," I admitted. "And besides, we've had some really great times this week, and I got to visit my secret place, so I'm happy."

"I guess we'll have to wait until next year to see it," said Ashley, looking bummed.

I smiled mischievously. "Well, maybe not," I said, grabbing my canvas for everyone to see. "This is what I spent the last few hours doing."

Everyone gathered around to admire the painting. I could tell how impressed they were, which made me happy.

"That is incredible!" said Delaney. The others murmured in agreement as they turned their marshmallows around in the fire.

I blushed. "Thanks, guys," I said. "I still have to put on a few more finishing touches since I'm leaving it as a present for the Huntleys. After all, we need to give them something, and it's not going to be a pinecone wreath, is it?" I couldn't resist teasing them a little.

"Ouch," joked Maren, clutching her heart. "You had to go there, didn't you?" We all giggled, knowing our silly fight was ancient history now.

"Will you have time to finish it?" asked Delaney, who couldn't help herself from worrying about timelines and deadlines.

"I'm going to have to make time before we go," I told her. "Maybe I can even finish it tonight if we're not out here too late?"

Ashley shook her head. "Fat chance," she said, grinning. "This is our last night here, and we're doing it sleepover-style!" A big smile spread across my face. I wouldn't have expected anything less.

The sun was starting to go down, and the sky was full of beautiful, insanely bright pinks and oranges. It reminded me of the moment we'd arrived — hard to believe the week was already coming to a close. "Anyone up for a toast?" I asked, holding my marshmallow skewer high. "Here's to our weeklong sleepover . . . and a vacation I'm never going to forget."

"And here's to you, Willow!" said Maren. "Thanks for inviting us along. I've traveled a lot, and this has been one of my fave trips yet. You and your parents are the best — and I guess your brother isn't too shabby, either."

We all giggled, and I thought about Winston and Jacob doing their thing in San Francisco. I'd barely given Jacob a second thought all week! It felt good to just focus on my friends and my family.

Ashley whipped out her phone. "Wait, before we toast, let me take a picture of us holding up our sticks," she said. At the looks on all of our faces, she quickly put her phone away. "I'm kidding!" Whew.

We all touched our glowing sticks together, then bit into our marshmallows. "Delish," said Delaney, giving everyone a thumbs-up.

At that moment, a firefly landed on Ashley's shirt. "Slug bug!" I said, hitting her arm lightly. "No one said we couldn't do it for real bugs, right?"

"*Oooh*, sneaky!" she said. "I'll have to get you back on the car ride tomorrow. Plus, I have to reclaim my title as Alphabet Soup Champion."

Maren covered her ears. "La-la-la-la," she sang, trying to drown us out. "Don't talk about the car ride! I don't want to think about leaving."

And neither did I. As far as I was concerned, spring break had been far too short! Maybe not everything had gone perfectly, and we could have used a few more days, for sure. But luckily, I knew this was far from the last adventure the Sleepover Girls were going to have together. From Whidbey to Valley View and everywhere in between, life was always more fun with my BFFs by my side.

Trustworthy Quiz

Can you rely on your friends to do the right thing?
And even more important, can they expect the same from
you? Take the quiz, add up your points, and see how
trustworthy you really are.

1. Your friend tells you a juicy secret. You promise not to
   tell anyone. This means:

   a) That I really won't tell anyone. But if I do spill the beans,
      I'll make them pinky-swear never to tell a soul. (2)

   b) I'll try, but I've been known to blab here and there. (3)

   c) My lips are sealed, superglue-style. (1)

2. You need money to go to the movies, but you already
   spent your allowance. You discover Mom sometimes
   hides cash in the cookie jar. What do you do?

   a) Take only the exact amount you need, and leave a
      note promising to pay it back. (2)

   b) Leave the money alone, and stay home from the
      movie. (1)

   c) Sneak a few bucks. She'll probably never notice. (3)

3. Your sister accidentally leaves her Facebook account
   open. What happens next?

a) It's super tempting to sneak a peek, but you close it out for her without looking. (1)

b) You post a message revealing her secret crush. (3)

c) You take a quick scroll through her messages folder and tease her about the posts later. (2)

4. When you get mad at one of your friends, you usually:

a) Talk to everyone about it but her. (3)

b) Tell her you're mad — and why you're mad! (1)

c) Hold it in for a while. But at some point, you fess up to what's bugging you. (2)

5. Every Tuesday you help your biology teacher clean the fish tanks after school. But when a friend says she has two free tickets for the newest vampire flick, it's pretty tempting. You:

a) Ask your friend to help you out in the biology lab. You'll offer to pay for tickets to see the movie another time. (1)

b) Leave the teacher a note that you'll clean the tank first thing in the morning. (2)

c) Feel a little guilty, but blow off the fishies. (3)

6. You find a $20 bill on the floor at a restaurant! You:

a) Look around to see who might have dropped it. If no one seems to be looking for the money, you can pocket it. (2)

b) Turn it in to the restaurant manager. (1)

c) Snatch it up immediately! (3)

7. How often do you break plans?

   a) Rarely if ever, unless an emergency pops up. (1)

   b) All the time! My mood changes a lot, and I can't be tied down to plans. (3)

   c) Sometimes, especially when a can't-miss opportunity comes along. (2)

8. What's one thing you wish you could change about yourself?

   a) Not being such a gossip. (3)

   b) Always being late. (2)

   c) Trusting others too much. (1)

9. You're totally stuck for a song to perform in the school talent show. You overhear a classmate rehearsing one that would be perfect for your voice. What do you do?

   a) Talk to the teacher to see if it's okay if two people do the same song. (2)

   b) See if your classmate will help you brainstorm another great tune. (1)

   c) Try to talk her out of performing the song. (3)

10. It's Tuesday, which means softball practice after school at 3:30. At 3:31, where are you?

a) On your way home to chill and watch some TV. You're just not in the mood to practice today! (3)

b) In uniform, on the field, and ready to go. (1)

c) Still in the locker room rushing to get ready. You are always late! (2)

11. One of your friends isn't the most reliable girl on the planet. When she's thirty minutes late to a smoothie date, your reaction is:

a) I'd better call to make sure she's okay. (1)

b) Smoothie to go, please! (3)

c) Ten more minutes, and then I'm out of here. (2)

12. You and a friend win tickets to meet your favorite indie rock band. At the concert, he snags the last signed poster and CD, which you totally wanted. When he forgets them in your mom's car, you:

a) Promise you'll give them back soon. once you scan in the poster and burn a copy of the CD. (2)

b) Call him right away to see when he'll pick them up. (1)

c) Keep them, and keep quiet. (3)

13. Your parents are going out for date night, which means you're allowed to have a friend come over! After your parents leave, another pal texts to see if she can join in the fun. You write back:

a) "Sorry, but I'm allowed to have only one friend over. Let's get together next time they go out." (1)

b) "Do you think you could leave before my parents get home? I'll be in big trouble if I get caught." (2)

c) "Only if you bring pizza and magazines!" (3)

14. Your sister finally lets you borrow her favorite shirt. You get a tiny stain on it. What do you do?

a) Frantically count your allowance. Maybe you can buy her a new one, and she'll never know the difference! (2)

b) Try to scrub out the stain and hope she won't notice. (3)

c) Fess up right away and offer to pay for dry-cleaning the shirt. (1)

15. When you take magazine quizzes, you:

a) Choose your answers honestly. After the quiz is complete, you check to see what they mean. (1)

b) Tend to peek at the answers before you're done taking the quiz. (3)

c) Try to pick the "right" answers to get the results you want! (2)

16. The most important quality I look for in a new friend is:

a) A forgiving nature. (3)

b) Reliability. (1)

c) A sense of fun. (2)

16 to 26 points: You are as trusty as can be! Everyone needs a friend who can be counted on. And that person is you! When a friend is crying, you offer a shoulder. When your friend has broccoli in her teeth, you're there with the mirror. When your parents need a babysitter, they can depend on you. You try really hard to keep your word.

27 to 37 points: Sure, you don't openly double-cross your friends. But sometimes your actions do let them down. Maybe you're always late. Or maybe you break plans at the last minute. If trust was a scale of one to ten, you'd be sitting at about six. There are tons of ways to be more trustworthy. Be more honest. Keep your promises. Don't go behind others' backs to do or say things. Put these ideas in practice, and your trustworthiness will grow.

38 to 48 points: You need a reliability boost! Right now your friendships may be on rocky ground. Without trust, it's hard for friends to confide in you or turn to you in times of need. Have you ever embarrassed a friend by telling a secret? Have you ever tattled just to get someone in trouble? Have you talked behind your friends' backs? If you've been guilty of any of these things, some relationship repair might be in order.

Note: This text was taken from *How Trustworthy Are You?* by Jen Jones (Capstone Press, 2012).

Can't get enough Sleepover Girls?
Check out the first chapter of

Maren's New Family

chapter One

"Maren!" came my mom's voice from downstairs for what seemed like the bazillionth time. Her voice was starting to get that tone, the one I knew meant I was skating on thin ice. "Time to grace us with your presence, please."

I knew I was in trouble, but I didn't care. I just pretended to be totally engrossed in the magazine I was reading, ignoring all the looks I was getting from my three best friends.

Never one to miss an opportunity to take charge, Delaney tapped her finger expectantly on her notepad.

"Time's up, Mar-Bear," she said, playfully throwing a pillow my way. "We've been holed up in your room for hours!"

"Yeah, I'm feeling a little trapped," said Ashley, looking up from the Instagram feed she was scrolling through on her phone. Ash was always finding new trends to blog about.

"We've got your back," Willow assured me, grabbing my hands. Reluctantly, I let her pull me off the bed.

As much as I hated to admit it, they were right. It was time to face the music and head downstairs, where my mom, her new boyfriend Gary (whom I'd secretly named "Garish," which means too bright or showy; it described him perfectly), and his kids were waiting to start our "family" game night.

Thankfully, my mom said I could invite my friends since they were like family to me. That was the only thing keeping me sane right now.

I folded my arms and pouted like a little kid. "Do I really have to do this?" I whined. "My mom acts like we're all going to be an instant happy little family."

I knew I was being a brat, but it was bad enough that Garish seemed to be stealing away all of my mom's free time. Now his kids were coming over too? Clearly my mom and Garish were more serious than I thought.

"Don't you think you're being a bit dramatic about this?" asked Delaney. "We're just playing games, not sending your mom down the aisle or anything."

"Thank the stars for that," I said, leading the charge out of my room. "Let's do this."

Once we made it downstairs, I saw that my mom had put a lot of effort into game night. There was a Twister mat in place of our usual tablecloth, and she'd put Oreos on a checkerboard in place of the playing pieces. Plus, my mom had made funny little signs using Scrabble tiles to describe the food, like Candyland Pops for the cake pops and Pick-Up Stix for the candy-coated pretzel rods. If I wasn't so annoyed I would be impressed.

Watching the other girls "ooh" and "ahh" over my mom's decorating, I had a tiny pang of guilt. Usually, my mom and I would have had a blast brainstorming and setting everything up together. But I'd been avoiding her for days, pouting about the entire event.

"Celeste outdid herself this time, huh?" Garish said, grinning from ear to ear. His bald head seemed to be gleaming under the overhead light.

I nodded, smiled weakly, and stuffed a cake pop in my mouth to avoid making conversation.

Willow swooped in, hoping to lessen an awkward moment and ease the obvious tension.

"She sure did," she said, helping herself to a fruity Monopoly mocktail. "Mrs. Taylor always knows how to get the party started! That must be where Maren gets it from."

My mom shot Willow a grateful look, then locked her eyes on me. "Maren, I think it's time you met Gary's children," she said, motioning toward the two kids play-fighting on the couch. They were dressed alike in some sort of striped nautical get-up. "This is Alice and Ace. They're in the second grade at Valley View Elementary."

As if it couldn't get any worse, they were twins! "Hi, guys," I said. "I didn't know they made matching outfits for boy-girl twins. How . . . cute."

Watching me struggle to be nice, Delaney stepped in to save the day. "Second grade? You might know my sister," she said to Alice and

Ace. "Gigi Brand? She's in fourth grade with Ms. Kirchner."

The twins kept right on tackling each other, as if they hadn't even heard Delaney. Garish cleared his throat, embarrassed. "Looks like they've still got plenty of energy to burn," he said. "So, on that note, who's ready to get their game on?"

My competitive spirit kicked in. "This girl," I said, raising my hand high. "As the reigning Trivial Pursuit champ, I believe I get to pick the first game. And that game is Pictionary!"

"Woo-hoo!" yelled Willow, always ready for anything that involved drawing or painting. She was a talented artist, so naturally, I snagged her for my team. Not so luckily, I also ended up with Garish and Alice. My mom, Ace, Delaney, and Ashley made up the other team.

While Garish set up the easel, my girls and I flopped onto our favorite spots on the sectional couch. My house was a second home to my friends. They'd slept over more times than I could ever try to count! It was part of our deal as the Sleepover Girls. Every Friday, we took turns hosting our weekly sleepovers. I lived for Fridays!

Ashley was up first at the easel, rocking flowered reading glasses for effect. "Dig in," my mom urged, passing the bowl full of drawing prompts at her. "First category: movie titles!"

Ash fished out her piece of paper and read it thoughtfully. She waited for Willow to turn the hourglass timer upside down. "And, go!" prompted Willow, chewing her long blond fishtail braid nervously.

Ashley eagerly started drawing something that kind of resembled an ice cube tray in a freezer. *The Big Chill*!" guessed my mom, but Ashley shook her head. She pointed at the ice cube tray, trying to drive home the hint. The team kept throwing out ideas: *Ice Age*! *The Ice Storm*!

It seemed like time was going to run out, but Ace came through in the clutch. *"Frozen*!" he yelled just as the timer ran out. Ashley started jumping up and down at his correct answer.

"Nailed it!" she said, high-fiving him.

"She should have drawn Elsa," sniffed Alice, rolling her eyes. "Who draws an ice cube tray?"

I wasn't about to have this little girl trash-talking any of my friends, even if they were on the other team. "Why don't you see if you can do better?" I said, handing the bowl to her.

Alice took the challenge, digging deep into the bowl. "No problem," she said, straightening her striped sailor skirt. Once the timer started, she started drawing a girl with a tiara next to an open book (or at least it kind of looked like a book). It didn't take me long to decipher the clues.

"*Princess Diaries*," I yelled. "Bam!"

"Way to go, Maren," said Garish, smiling at me.

My happiness quickly faded. I looked the other way, only to find Alice doing a little victory dance and shaking her booty in my face. Charming! Avoiding my mom's stare, I cleared my throat and got up to hand the bowl to Delaney. "Your turn, D."

I may have been on Garish's team in the literal sense, but I was so not on Team Garish.

Four BEST FRIENDS plus one weekly tradition equals a whole lot of FUN!

Join in by following Delaney, Maren, Ashley, and Willow's adventures in the Sleepover Girls series. Every Friday, new memories are made as these sixth-grade girls gather together for crafts, fashion, cooking, and of course girl talk! Grab your pillow, settle in, and get to know the Sleepover Girls.

Want to throw a sleepover party your friends will never forget?

Let the Sleepover Girls help!
The Sleepover Girls Craft titles
are filled with easy recipes, crafts,
and other how-tos combined with
step-by-step instructions and colorful
photos that will help you throw the best
sleepover party ever! Grab all eight of
the Sleepover Girls Craft titles before
your next party so you can create
unforgettable memories.

sleepover Girls crafts
Amazing
OUTDOOR ART
You Can Make and Share

sleepover Girls crafts
Awesome
RECIPES
You Can Make and Share

sleepover Girls crafts
Colorful
CREATIONS
You Can Make and Share

sleepover Girls crafts
Fab
FASHIONS
You Can Make and Share

sleepover Girls crafts
Paper
PRESENTS
You Can Make and Share

sleepover Girls crafts
Spa
PROJECTS
You Can Make and Share

sleepover Girls crafts
Super
SCIENCE PROJECTS
You Can Make and Share

sleepover Girls crafts
Unique
ACCESSORIES
You Can Make and Share

About the Author:
Jen Jones

Los Angeles-based author and
journalist Jen Jones speaks fluent
tween. She has written more than
seventy books about celebrities,
crafting, cheerleading, fashion, and
just about any other obsession a
girl in middle school could have —
including her popular *Team Cheer!* and
Sleepover Girls series for Capstone.

About the Illustrator: Paula Franco

Paula was born and raised in Argentina. She studied Illustration, animation, and graphic design at Instituto Superior de Comunicacion Visual in Rosario, Argentina. After graduating, Paula moved to Italy for two years to learn more about illustration. Paula now lives in Argentina and works as a full-time illustrator. Her work is published worldwide. She spends a lot of her free time wandering around bookshops and playing with her rescued dogs.